THE CHURCH MICE AT CHRISTMAS

Graham Oakley

M

MACMILLAN CHILDREN'S BOOKS

ISBN 0-333-32483-8

First published 1980 by
MACMILLAN CHILDREN'S BOOKS
A division of Macmillan Publishers Limited
London and Basingstoke
Associated companies throughout the world

Picturemac edition published 1981
Reprinted 1982, 1983, 1984, 1985

Printed in Hong Kong

One morning a few days before Christmas, Arthur and Humphrey, the leaders of the church mice, were in the porch admiring the Christmas tree.

"It would be jolly nice to have a party," said Arthur suddenly. "A real Christmas party with paper hats and crackers and games and things."

"Oh yes!" cried Humphrey. "And mince pies and trifle and custard and blancmange and cream and jelly."

So it was all settled.

The first thing they had to do was to think of a way of earning some money because parties can be expensive. That puzzled them, until Arthur happened to glance at the notice board. "That's it!" he cried. "We'll raffle something."

They were just trying to think what the "something" could be when Sampson, the church cat, appeared. The mice looked at him, and then they looked at each other and smiled.

They made quite sure that they stood well out of Sampson's reach when they told him they had decided to raffle him.

But in the end they managed to convince him they were doing him a favour really because whoever won him would *certainly* be a cat lover and treat him with *great* respect and take him to a *lovely* home and give him an *enormous* dinner, and anyway he could come back to the vestry as soon as he liked. So they went ahead with the raffle at once. . .

. . . and soon the day of the draw arrived.

It went very well and everything happened exactly as Arthur and Humphrey had predicted.

Well, perhaps not exactly, but Sampson was fairly philosophical about it. "After all," he said to himself as he slunk back to the vestry an hour or so later, "any cat that's stupid enough to take a vow never to harm mice deserves what he gets."

When he arrived, the mice were still discussing how best to spend the raffle money.

Later that evening, however, the raffle winners discovered that their prize had run away.
But they weren't too worried because they knew where they would find him, roughly.

And Humphrey showed them precisely. He said he was sorry that the prize hadn't given
satisfaction and although he couldn't, under any circumstances, refund their ticket
money, he was able to offer them the vestry dustpan instead, which was much better
value than a mere cat even if the handle was missing.

But the couple preferred Sampson. They tried to wheedle him out with winning smiles and honeyed words, but Sampson wouldn't be wheedled.

So eventually, despite what Humphrey had said about not giving refunds, they took their money and went home. The mice were really depressed about this because without the money there would be no party. Humphrey muttered that though it wasn't in his nature to criticise, there was a certain whiskery, ginger individual who would do well to look up the word *selfish* in the dictionary. But he didn't say it loud enough for Sampson to hear.

To cheer themselves up, Arthur and Humphrey decided to go across to the vicarage to watch television. On the way they racked their brains to think of another way to make some money, but without success. Later on, however, they saw something which sparked off an idea.

And next day they rounded up the mice with the loudest voices. They spent the whole morning practising their scales and the whole afternoon sorting out the pronunciation of Wenceslas, and by the time it was dark, they were ready.

Carol singing had seemed a really good plan
in the vestry. . . .

But as Humphrey said afterwards, "Everybody knows that the best laid schemes o' mice an' thingummies gang aft a-gley."

And those who didn't were learning – fast. Arthur and Humphrey fled through a shop
door . . .

. . . and inside they tried a rather clever ruse. It would have worked, too, if a customer hadn't thought they would make such lovely little stocking-fillers.

From then on it was just one thing after another. Fortunately, Arthur kept his head . . .

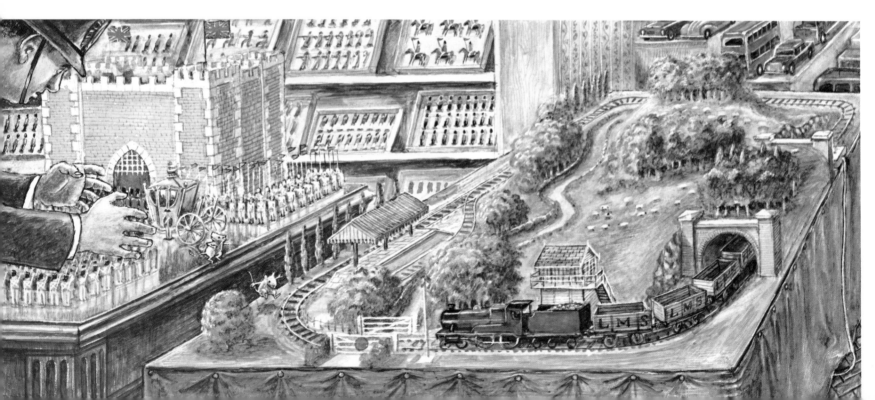

. . . and managed to get them aboard a passing train. Humphrey complained that they should have enquired where it was going first, but Arthur said they would find out soon enough. They never did.

But just when it looked as if they had come to the end,
Arthur spotted the very thing for a quick getaway. . .

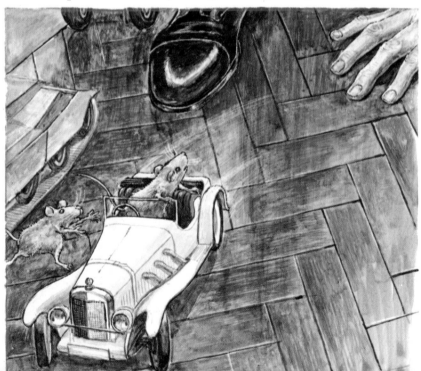

. . . although it turned out to be a pretty close-run thing. Once outside, the mice all met up again and managed to slip away unnoticed into the crowd.

The journey back to the vestry was dreadful. Everyone was gloomy because of the failure of the expedition, and it didn't help matters to have to listen to Humphrey explaining his new theory about how Christmas Day should change places with August Bank Holiday so that people wouldn't have to tramp through the snow to do their Christmas shopping.

It took ages for them to get their wind back, but when they had, Arthur announced that since they hadn't made a single penny out of their carol singing, there wouldn't be a party after all. At this, the mice looked so miserable that Arthur, after a few moments' thought, told them they should cheer up because he still had a very pleasant surprise in store for them.

After that, he and Humphrey whispered together for a long time. Then, as quietly as possible, they filled a paper bag with odds and ends from the choirboys' lockers, woke Sampson and tiptoed out of the vestry while nobody was looking. Outside, Arthur assured them that they would find whatever else they needed in the parson's garden shed.

On the way back to the vestry a most wonderful thing happened to them. Even Humphrey was speechless for two seconds. Then he said, "Good evening, Father Christmas sir. I am Humphrey, and what I want for Christmas is a quadrophonic record player, a quartz watch, four ounces of jelly babies, a pair of two-tone football boots, a—"

"And what I would like. . ." began Arthur.

"—transistor radio," continued Humphrey, "a dozen walnut whips. . .

. . . the *Beano* Annual, a yo-yo, two pounds of fudge, an electric guitar, a—"

"And what I would. . ." began Arthur.

"—colour television," Humphrey continued, "six boxes of cheese spread, a cuckoo clock, a pocket calculator and a packet of custard creams."

"And what I. . ." began Arthur.

"Well, that will do for now," said Humphrey, "because the sergeant is obviously in a hurry to give you his list. So if Your Worship will just make a note of my address —" and he shouted it out, very slowly so that there could be no mistake. "Right then," he finished, "we'll expect Your Highness at nine o'clock tonight, sharp. Carry on, sergeant."

They decided they might as well go on pretending to be Father Christmas even though the real one was now going to visit them, because it would amuse the mice and fill up the time until he arrived. Unfortunately, it wasn't the mice who seemed to find them amusing. . .

. . . so their return to the vestry was anything but the very pleasant surprise that Arthur
had promised . . .

. . . though they made up for it by telling the mice about their meeting with Father
Christmas and explaining that he would be coming to the vestry at nine o'clock.
Everyone started to get ready at once.

Meanwhile, a reward for the persons who had helped to capture the burglar had arrived at Wortlethorpe Police Station, and the sergeant, who had heard Humphrey shouting out his address, promised to deliver it himself.

Back in the vestry, it wasn't long before everything was spick and span, and by the time the church clock struck nine, the mice were ready and waiting.

At the same moment in Wortlethorpe Police Station, the sergeant was struck with a brilliant idea. If great detectives can wear disguises to catch villains, he thought to himself, why can't I? So he borrowed the burglar's Father Christmas outfit, and when he looked in the mirror he scarcely recognised himself. "It's a stroke of genius," he muttered. "I'll be a chief inspector before you can say Sherlock Holmes!"

In the vestry the mice heard the clock strike quarter past nine, and Arthur and Humphrey started to get worried. At the police station the sergeant was just setting off on his rounds, and as he had to pass the church, he decided to deliver the mice's reward.

When the clock struck half past nine, Arthur and Humphrey began to fear for their safety. Humphrey started to stammer that Father Christmas was probably having trouble with his reindeer or something, but the mice were in no mood for excuses.

And by a quarter to ten, the mood in the vestry was very ugly indeed. Sampson was about to step in and do something about it when suddenly the door creaked open and. . .

For a long time after Father Christmas had gone, the mice just sat and stared, murmuring things like "Gosh," and "Golly," and "Crumbs." Then, with shrieks of excitement, they all rushed to see what he had brought them.

What they saw was everything that anybody could possibly want for a Christmas party.

And what a party they had. It was good enough to make Humphrey forget all about quadrophonic record players and yo-yos and things. In fact it was so good that they were all ill for three days after it and when it was over there was enough left for the choirboys to have a party of their own and be ill for three days as well. Even after that the mice were still able to find a box of crystallized fruits, a tin of asparagus and a jar of pickled walnuts, and since it was the season of goodwill to all men, they decided to give these to the parson. But then Humphrey informed them that years and years of intensive scientific research had proved conclusively that parsons don't like crystallized fruits. So they kept those, and had a feast on New Year's Eve, just to round off the year nicely.